A Novel in Stories by

Derek McCormack

DARK RIDES

The publisher acknowledges the assistance of the Canada Council.

CANADIAN CATALOGUING IN PUBLICATION DATA
McCormack, Derek
Dark rides
"A Ken Sparling Book"
ISBN 1-896356-06-0
I. Title.
PS8575.C67D37 1996 C813'.54 C95-933383-5
PR9199.3.M33D37 1996

Published by Gutter Press,
118 Peter Street, Suite #1, Toronto, Ontario M5V 2G7
http://www.io.org/~gutter/
Represented in Canada by the Literary Press Group
Distributed in Canada by General Publishing,
30 Lesmill Rd, Don Mills, Ontario
Distributed in the U.S. by Distributed Art Publishers (D.A.P.),
636 Broadway, 12th Floor, New York, NY 10012
(Tel 212.473 5119 Fax 212.673 2887). To order, call 1 800 338 BOOK

Manufactured in Canada by Coach House Printing
Third Printing, April 1997

ACKNOWLEDGEMENTS

I wish to thank the Canada Council for financial support.

Many thanks to the staff of Book City, Elizabeth Brick of the Herschell Carrousel Factory Museum, Chris Chambers, Linda Cobon of the Canadian National Exhibition Records and Archives, Sean Gaherty, Sam Hiyate, Elwood H. Jones (who graciously arranged for me to print several photos that had already appeared in his book, *Winners: 150 Years of the Peterborough Exhibition*), Suzanne Leslie, John Lutman of the J.J. Talman Regional Collection at the University of Western Ontario, Cynthia and Murray McCormack, Melissa McCormack, Yvonne Matchett of the Peterborough Agricultural Society, Christopher Paulin, D'Arcy Salzmann, Oliver Salzmann, Todd Skitch, Ken Sparling, Chris Waters, Deborah Wilton.

Special thanks to Esther Mazakian, a tireless reader. And to Jason McBride, who supported me and advised the project from the get go.

The following stories were published previously:

"When In Rome", *sub-TERRAIN*, Fall 1995

"The Crepe-Hanger", *The Malahat Review*, Spring 1996

"Dead Man's Curve", *Ink*, Winter 1995

"Victor Mature", *WRIT*, Number 27

"Ex" (under the title "The Marrying Kind"), *McGill Street Magazine,* Spring 1995

"Buoy" (under the title "Antibody: An Autobiography"), *Grain,* Fall 1992

"Love Lies Deep", *The Quarterly*, Number 30

"Hands", *The Peterborough Review*, Winter/Spring 1995

"Cattle Call", *Blood & Aphorisms*, Summer 1995

"Passing On", *Shift*, Summer 1993

For my family.

TABLE OF CONTENTS

ALLIS-CHALMERS

BACKWARD

I hid in my room. Scrubbed sand on my pecker and belly and bum. I was trying to kill the germs but my hands kept shaking and then it hit me. The man's word. *Combust.*

*

The ground smoked. The police come by. Also a man in a black suit who talked to Dad and the firemen.

I said to him, You find out who done it?

He said nobody did it. He said germs lived in our hay and rotted it and the rotting made it hot. He said it was chemical. He called it something.

What do you mean germs? I said.

They're invisible, he said. You can't get rid of them.

*

The roof crashed and sparks flew up. A fire truck roared in. Behind it come a truck loaded up with guys.

Dad shook me by the shoulders. He said, What were you doing? He said, Were you fooling with caps?

I started to cry. My snot all black from smoke.

*

Dad dove into the smoke. Then him and the horses come barrelling out. McNaughtons drove down from their farm and then the Pointers run down from theirs and they all got a water line going between the barn and the well. Me holding buckets while Ted Pointer pumped.

Ted shouted, You didn't see anyone did you?

I shook my head. The flames went high as pines.

*

The sun was burning something fierce. The grass pricked my feet. I tiptoed to the stoop and plopped down on the porch glider, picked hayseed out of my hair and off my shoulders. Then I heard it. A whoosh. The barn blurred. Flames sawed the roof.

*

Ted Pointer was lying at the back of the hayloft. How's my buddy? he said.

The hay was cooking. I stepped out of my overalls and crouched. His pecker was jerking itself upright. Blue veins, green veins, veins the colour of red cabbage. I put the end of it in my mouth. Horses snorting below. Then he lifted my head and rolled on top of me and started rubbing his body against mine. His forehead dripping into my eyes.

TREASURE TRAIL

I had to stand in a cornfield, arms spread scarecrow-style. Straw hat, cord suit. Wormy husks up my sleeves and down my neck.

Just past sundown a bunch of people rode by on a hay wagon.

A gal with a megaphone said, "Rumour has it Wendell hid out in these parts. He lived on berries and innocent children...."

I hollered and charged the wagon. Kids shrieked. Parents hugged them, pointed at me and laughed.

Every half-hour another wagonload rumbled by. At 11 the driver drove down alone.

"I'm Pete," he said.

"Good for you," I said.

*

The megaphone gal gabbed about ghosts and ghouls as the first wagonload of the night rolled away.

I had a smoke. I jacked off. I wandered to the edge of the field and scaled the snake fence. Wading through tallgrass I tripped on a wheel. It was sticking straight up out of the ground. I found another one about five feet away. I began digging with my hands.

In the wagon Pete asked how I'd gotten dirty.

"You tell the boss and I'll kill you," I said.

He traced an X on his chest. "Cross my heart."

"There's a hay rake buried out there." I pointed.

"So?"

"So?" I said. "People'll pay lots for shit like that. It's an antique."

*

Next shift I took a shovel. I managed to unearth the rake's seat and prongs. But I had to keep running back to the cornfield to spook brats. One kid in snow pants started bawling. I rushed her. She grabbed my sleeve and chomped down on my fingers.

"Goddammit!" I yelled.

The boss was waiting by the barn after work. "Young man this is a family ride," he said. "Any more cussing and you're out of here! History! Understand?"

I hung my head. Out the corner of my eye I

watched Pete park and lock the wagon.

*

"What a dope," Pete said next night. We passed a pasture planted with cardboard tombstones. "He didn't even ask what happened."

"Tell me something pal," I said. "The boss let you keep the keys to this thing?"

He shrugged. "Sure."

"Let's say you wanted to borrow it."

"No problem."

"Suppose you didn't ask."

The Haunted Barn, The Haunted Mini-Golf Course, The Haunted Snack Shack. Lights were out at the boss's house. A jack-o'-lantern asleep on the stoop.

*

Next shift I dug down to the rake's tongue. The soil beneath it was froze. I climbed onto the seat and jacked off.

The wagon rumbled closer.

I jammed my dick into my cords and ran. My right foot slid into a groundhog hole. I tumbled. The wagon's headlights grew bright.

"It seems the scarecrow's gone," said the megaphone gal. "Where could it be?"

"Here I am!" I yelled. I rose and staggered toward the wagon. "Here I am you fucking little bitch!"

Later on Pete idled the wagon beneath a rag-stuffed dummy dangling from an elm. He peeled off my boot and sock.

I faked a sob. "What am I gonna do?" I said. "I needed this job."

"This sucks," Pete said. "You hurt yourself making money for Mr. Moore. One little mistake and he's all over you." He slammed the gear stick into drive. "I'll help you get that rake," he said. "Just say when."

*

Halloween night I knocked out two sections of the snake fence. Near midnight Pete showed up in the wagon. We backed up to the rake, roped its rear beam to the wagon's hitch.

"I reckon it'll take one good tug," Pete said jumping into the cab.

The engine revved, the rope tensed, the rake groaned. *Crack!*–the beam snapped. Prongs and chunks of wood flew into weeds.

Pete leapt out. "Did we get it?" he said.

"Get it?" I screamed. "You fucking idiot you broke it!"

I slugged him in the kisser. He hit the dirt.

"C'mon candyass!" I screamed. "Get up and fight!"

Blood trickled from his nose.

"Pete?" I nudged him with my boot. Straddling his hips I pushed his sweater up to his arm pits. I listened to his heartbeat. I licked his nipples. I unbuckled his belt.

PLUMBING
INSTALLED BY
WATER ST
PETERBOROUGH

WHEN IN ROME

Disguised in a wig Caligula roamed the streets of Rome, stabbing soldiers and dumping their bodies down sewers...

In October my History teacher assigned presentations. My topic–the Emperor Caligula.

I asked the school librarian where I could find information. She brought me *The Twelve Caesars* by Suetonius. A clothbound edition made in Great Britain.

"This may not be removed from the library," she said, "but you're free to use it here."

I sat at a reading table and started making notes. Dates of Caligula's electoral reforms, military campaigns. How many consulships he took. Then I saw this:

"Caligula was accused of homosexual relations, both active and passive, with Marcus Lepidus, and Mnester the comedian, and various foreign hostages...."

My cheeks flushed. I reread the sentence. I copied it out in capitals.

Caligula would force men to wear short tunics and run alongside his chariot...

The next day I lunched in a carrel. I read how Caligula annexed parts of Rome for his palace. City blocks became hallways, tenements became suites. In one suite he opened a brothel. Men could go and sleep with the boys and married women who worked there.

Boys. My penis ballooned. Hands pocketed I rushed to the Tech hall washroom.

Caligula would invite men to supper, forgetting he'd murdered them already...

When I got back to the library my books were gone. I ransacked my knapsack. I checked under my chair.

Someone snickered. A guy in the opposite carrel rose and waved Suetonius at me.

I walked around, heart trilling. The guy was sitting with another fellow who started reading my notes:

"Caligula was a queer accused of fucking every queer in Rome and als–"

I grabbed them. "Please give me the book," I said.

The first guy grinned and tossed it on the desk. Pressing its right side he yanked its left, splitting the spine.

Age eighteen Caligula loved watching tortures and executions...

I handed the book in to the librarian. The librarian dragged me to see the principal. I got detention for three weeks. After school I swept the gym. Student council members were there, stringing orange and black streamers between the lights.

Caligula surveying a lineup of convicts: "Kill every man between the bald one and that short one!"

I bused to the Peterborough Public Library and signed out another copy of *The Twelve Caesars.* All the way home I read. Every day Caligula ate doses of twenty-three poisons to build up his resistance. He wrote two books–one listed poisons and their effects, the other the names of people he'd poisoned. His own father died with foaming lips and dark blotches on his body.

Some convicts were stabbed forty or fifty times...

After supper Mom and Dad went to a movie. I nibbled a daffodil bulb, sucked petals from a potpourri. I fixed a rubbing alcohol and Coca-Cola cocktail. Caligula liked the taste of pearls dissolved in vinegar. I stirred an aspirin into my drink. It gave me pins and needles in my hands and feet. My eyes started focusing without me.

Some convicts were manacled and tossed into the Tiber...

Juiced up on poison I lit out for the school. Leaves cartwheeling down the sidewalk before me.

I slipped into the foyer, past kids bobbing for apples. In the gym a band was strumming a country song under the basketball hoop.

Others were dragged naked through the streets until stones sliced them and their bowels plopped out...

I hunted the fools who'd destroyed my library book. Through the cafeteria, the teacher's lunchroom, the parking lot. In the men's locker room I found three lugs straddling urinals.

"Check out the faggot," one lug said.

"You a fag?" said another.

"Hate me," I said, "so long as you fear me!"

They wrenched my arm and pulled my hair and dragged me on my knees into a stall. Piss frothing in the toilet.

"Thirsty fag?"

"I'm warning you," I said.

In I went. My forehead banged porcelain. I screamed as they pulled me out. I shut my mouth before they dunked me again.

THE CREPE-HANGER

I dumped the eye shadows on my bed–Midnight Mauve, Granite Gray, Satiny Silver.

"I'll look like a fairy!" Jack said. He huffed, lay down, unbuttoned his shirt. With my finger I smeared shadows on his neck, his chin. His lips.

My penis shot up. I crossed my legs.

Carved turnips grimacing from stoops. Maple trees red as clown wigs. I had on a lab coat and stethoscope. Jack in a Salvation Army suit, hair teased and greened with paint powder.

Jeckyll and Hyde.

"Happy fucking Halloween," Jack mumbled.

A sheeted ghost hung from the Powells' porch-light. Paula answered the door, a cat in cat-pattern slipover and silk whiskers.

"You must be Jack!" she said. "Happy Halloween!"

Black and orange serpentines crisscrossed the drawing room ceiling. Paula introduced us to her folks and some girls from out of town. The rest of the guests we knew. Gerry McBride was a jack-o'-lantern. Muslin stretched over a wire cage.

"Hey Jack," he said, "where's your costume?"

"Shut up pumpkin boy."

Mrs. Powell clapped. "How about a game?"

She split us into teams, placed us on opposite sides of a white sheet hanging in a doorway. All lights off. The other team flicked on a flashlight. A shadow loomed up on the sheet–broad shoulders, porcupine hair....

"Jack!" I yelled. I won a Life Savers roll garnished with a crepe-ruff bow tie.

They sent up Gerry the jack-o'-lantern next. The beam pierced the costume's muslin, silhouetted its frame. An X-ray of God knows what.

We went down to the cellar. On the ceiling skull-and-crossbones string-'em-outs, on the walls crepe moss. A banner over the buffet: YE OLDE PIRATE'S CAVE.

Paula pointed to the food. "We've got treasure chests–" She held up a platter of triple-decker brown bread sandwiches. "Pieces of eight–" Chocolate-chip cookies with gold frosting. "Ices, candies, cider...."

Jack held up a plate of chocolate croquettes. "What're these?" he said. "Pirate turds?"

Mr. Powell carried in a tin tub brimming with water and apples. Mrs. Powell in tow with towels.

"Who wants to go first?" he said. "Derek? Dan? Gerry?"

"Oh for pete's sake," Jack said. He shucked his blazer, knelt at the tub. A deep breath and *splash!* He came up empty-mouthed. Next dip the powder in his hair became an emerald paint slick. He jerked up. "Get this crap out of my eyes!" he yelled.

Paula rushed him upstairs. Ten minutes later she led him down. His make-up gone. Eyes crazed with veins.

"Can you see all right?" I said.

He flashed me the finger. "Can you?"

Each girl peeled a long strip of skin from an apple. Diane threw her peel over her shoulder. It fell into an S-shape on the floor.

"S!" Mrs. Powell shouted. "Your husband's initial will be S!"

I sidled up to Paula. There was a smudge of colour on her lower lip. Midnight Mauve.

I froze. She flung her peel.

J.

I glanced at Jack. His eyes were fixed on Paula. Paula clutched my shoulder, blushed.

"Oh my God," she said, "I can't believe it, it's a–"

"It's not!" I said. "It's a squiggle! It's just a squiggle!" I kicked the peel. Now it was a squiggle.

Nobody spoke.

I stomped upstairs, burst outside, sat on the curb at the end of the drive. Leaves shocked on lawns. Apples pulped on the pavement.

Jack hunkered down beside me. "What the hell is going on?" he said.

"Don't act all innocent!" I said. "I know what you and Paula were doing in the bathroom!"

"I just kissed her!" he said. "She's cute. We were sitting there. I just kissed her."

I jumped up and bolted. Jack-o'-lanterns smashed on the street. A triangle eye. Half a grin. Trees bandaged with toilet tissue.

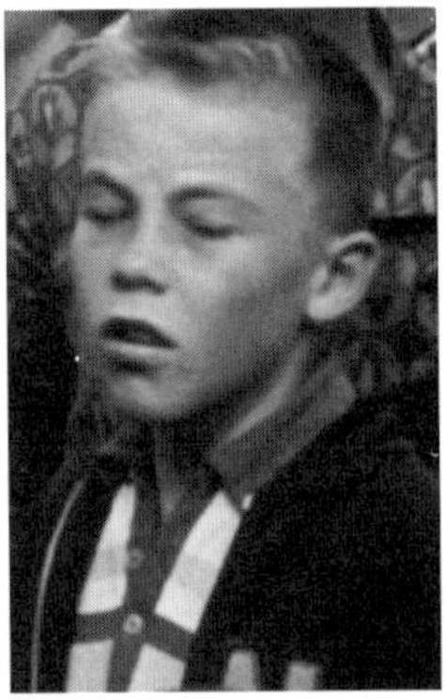

DEAD MAN'S CURVE

"Dead is Graham Porter, age twenty-two."

I turn up the radio.

*

I've only known one dead guy. Jonathan Worth. I sat two rows behind him in Grade 10 Geography. All through class I'd lean sideways and study him. Black hair squared across his neck. Bum wedged between the bars on his chair.

One Valentine's Day I tried sending him a carnation. Student Council was selling them to raise money for dances. I paid my dime and the Social Convener gave me an enclosure card.

"Fill out her name and home form," he said.

"Do I have to sign it?"

*

I clear off the table and iron my good clothes. Black suit, black tie, white shirt. A handkerchief I bought at the Sally Ann. It's white with a stencil-blue monogram. H.D.C. Whoever that is.

*

Henderson's held Jonathan's wake from 6 to 9 on a Wednesday evening. I showed up with ten minutes to go. The coat rack half empty. Mr. Henderson sat at a desk beside it.

"Would you care to make a donation?" he said. He passed me a pocket Bible. It had a red cover with gold lettering.

I gave him two bits.

"God bless," he said nudging the register at me.

I signed it "Friend of the Deceased".

*

I hang up my ironing and then dash downstreet. The sun's history, the temperature's plunging. I peer into Henderson's but nothing moves. A COME AGAIN sign hanging on the door.

At Jaye's I buy an *Examiner*. Graham Porter's front-page.

"Plowed his snowmobile into barbed wire," Mr. Jaye says. "Clotheslined him."

Three wrinkled eggs and a bottle of Jack

Daniels in my fridge. I pour myself a shot, then open the paper to Graham's obituary.

I tear out his photo. He's wearing a graduation robe. Knees at three o'clock, chest at noon, head up and out.

I file him in my Bible with the other guys. One electrocuted, two shot, two drowned. One guy had a heart attack.

*

Jonathan fishtailed trying to merge off the highway. The car hit a Hydro box. His head pierced the windshield. Mr. Henderson tweezed every shard of glass from his face. He disguised the scars with base. I rubbed a little of it off at the wake.

"Shit." I spun around. The room was empty save for an old couple on a loveseat. They nodded. I turned back. I stroked Jonathan's fingers and lips and the birthmark beneath his left eyebrow. My groin flush against the casket. Mouth dry as dust.

RIDE 'EM COWB
CANADIAN KIDDIE RIDES CO
RODEO KING CORRAL
TICKETS ACCEPTED HERE
TICKETS ACCEPTED HERE

VICTOR MATURE

Hugh pulled me to the ground and kissed me. Lips, nipples, navel. He yanked off my jeans to continue.

He swallowed, then straddled up my chest. Gripping my ears he fucked my mouth, yodelling like Roy Rogers when he came.

An Angus bull answered back. It snorted and hoofed dirt about a hundred yards away.

"We got ourselves an audience!" Hugh said, still holding my ears.

"Jesus Christ," I said. I fumbled backward, boxers around my knees, belt buckle rattling. "It's okay it's okay," I whispered to the cow.

Suddenly Hugh screamed "Soo-eee!" and hightailed it past me.

The bull moaned and charged.

Hugh hurdled the fence and collapsed laughing.

I vaulted over. My left ankle landed sideways on a chunk of cement.

*

In Emergency a nurse stripped me and threaded my arms through a hospital gown. She shot morphine in my butt. My ankle stopped screaming. My head started humming.

A man breezed in and picked up my chart. "I'm Dr. Ogilvie," he said. "Why don't you tell me what happened?"

"Me and Hugh were fooling around. I think I broke something."

He flipped through forms. "And Hugh is?"

"My pal," I said. Or thought I said. I couldn't be sure. I repeated it louder.

The doctor nodded and neared. Lights in my eyes, wood on my tongue. He rolled me toward the wall and scraped a fingernail down my behind. "What exactly were you boys doing?" he said.

"You know," I chuckled. "Messing around."

He stared down over his bifocals. I checked beneath me. Soil and hayseed matted on the white paper sheet.

"Be honest son," he said. "Were you with a girl?"

I said, "Why would I want a girl?"

Snapping on rubber gloves he combed through my pubic hair. Next he squeezed my testicles and pinched my penis.

"Actually that's working pretty good," I said.

*

When my folks got there I told them I'd been exploring the old cement works. "I fell through a landing," I said. "Took a half-hour to drag myself to the road."

The doctor told them I was stable physically but troubled mentally. "There are things your son confided," he said. He promised to send a summary to our G.P.

*

Hugh shinned up the drainpipe to the overhang outside my room. I rolled out of bed to meet him.

"You okay?" he said.

"Well I've got a hundred pounds of plaster on my foot."

He pressed his palm against the screen, trapping no-see-ums underneath. "I'm sorry," he said. He stuck out his lower lip. I let him crawl inside. He tipped me onto the mattress.

"Listen a sec," I said.

He fell on top of me, nibbled at my nose.

"Hugh the doctor knows."

He froze.

I shoved him off me. "What are we going to do?"

"There's nothing we can do is there?"

I turned away, my alarm clock tsking from my dresser, Dad sawing logs down the hall.

*

I started tacking Rita Hayworth photos over my desk. I took the girlie playing cards from Dad's sock drawer and stashed them underneath my pillow for Mom to find.

And I got a girlfriend. Lori Kelly. First day of school she volunteered to help me between classes. Carrying my books, holding my crutches.

After a week I invited her over for a thank-you supper. Mom laid out her bone china. Wine glasses for the adults, juice glasses for the two of us.

*

I took Lori to a show. Thugs knocked down Victor Mature. Victor Mature scrambled up, blood rilling out his nose. Derricks pumping crude behind him.

Lori webbed my hand through hers.

There was a whoop from somewhere behind us. I spun around but saw nothing. The picture flickering in people's eyeglasses.

"I'll be right back," I said.

I hobbled to the aisle and headed for the men's room. White lights, white porcelain, white tile. Shoe prints like dance steps on the floor.

Hugh was smoking by the urinals. He stepped

forward and gripped my shoulder. His other hand went down my spine.

I pulled back, stumbled, hit the hand dryer.

A toilet flushed. A sliding bolt. A man emerged from a stall and peered over at us.

Hugh wiped his lips with his sleeve. “Evenin’,” he said.

The man shot us a backward glance on his way out.

“Good going,” I said.

Hugh pulled me close. His eyelashes tickled mine. He said, “This is how much I care.”

A burning barn. Chickens flying helter-skelter, horses bucking against smoke. With a wet blanket draped over his head Victor Mature ran into the blaze. I slipped into my seat, hairs coiled on my tongue, pants damp against my thighs.

“Are you okay?” Lori said.

I nodded. “Fine,” I said. “What’s happening?”

She touched my wrist. Victor Mature’s family was cheering, cheeks smeared with grime, ashes snowing down around.

STARGAZE

From Peterborough I took the Greyhound. I checked into Toronto General Hospital. My room was a bed, a chair, a closet. A barred window. Streetcars sparked past in the night.

*

First thing in the morning I was sitting in Dr. Vine's office.

"Age?" he said.

"Eighteen," I said. "Sir."

He scribbled on my chart. "How long have you been aware of your inversion?"

I breathed deep. "Eighteen years."

In the examining room I stripped and stretched out on a gurney. He girded my shins and arms, rolled an electric generator up to me. Taped electrodes to my penis and scrotum.

He said, "I'd like you to describe your fantasies involving men."

I shut my eyes. I spoke about kissing Gary Cooper's lips and nipples and stomach and–

Dr. Vine shocked me.

Back in my room I cupped my balls in my palm. Legs cramped. After a couple hours I signed out at the nurses' station and went down to the street.

The July sun. I shuffled north, past Queen's Park and Victoria University. At the Royal Ontario Museum I bought a ticket and wandered into an auditorium where people sat in dentists' chairs under a plaster dome. The usher seated me as the house lights died.

Over loudspeakers: "Welcome to the Milky Way."

Constellations brightened overhead–the Pleiades, Cepheus, Andromeda–

The auditorium seemed to spin. I gasped.

*

Come morning Dr. Vine strapped me down and hooked me up and showed me photographs of naked hulks with brush-cuts flexing their biceps.

I glanced from them to him. He was drumming his fingertips against the pictures, nails yellow, uncut. My penis limp.

"You're not concentrating," he said. He lined the pictures up on an easel. He ripped the electrodes off my privates and pressed them to my temples.

I blacked out.

*

I walked to the planetarium. Sat near the projector. It was dumbbell-shaped, fifteen feet long. Lying lengthwise it projected the night skies of the northern and southern hemispheres. Then it tilted. At a twenty-degree angle it shot out images of the planets. It tilted again and suddenly the sun filled the dome.

*

In the morning in Dr. Vine's office. I took off my clothes.

"You're extremely tense," he said. "Can you tell me why?"

"Because you really hurt me yesterday," I said.

"You're generalizing." He wheeled the generator closer. He wired my temples. "Your behaviour," he said. "Your behaviour is what hurts. Isn't that so?"

"Yes but I'm not sure–"

He ordered me to think men. Nude men.

"I can't, I'm too nervous."

"Close your eyes *now!*"

*

I came to in my room, my pillow bloody. I'd bitten my tongue.

At the Greyhound depot I bought popsicles. My lips were grape when I pulled into Peterborough.

I tramped home to bed. Clouds blanking out the stars.

*

Didn't catch a wink till dawn. My alarm went off and I ignored it. Sometime after noon the telephone rang. I picked it up.

It was Dr. Vine. "Admitting told me you'd checked out," he said.

My legs cramped.

"I'm expecting you bright and early tomorrow."

"No it's okay," I stammered. "I think I'm cured."

"If you're not here in the morning I'll be forced to contact your parents. Or the police."

I threw on some clothes and dashed downstreet. The bookstore had nothing. Likewise Hampton's Novelty Shop. At Turnbull's Department Store I snatched up a celestial map and a copy of *The Amateur Astronomer's Guide.*

"You been to the Ex?" the saleslady said. She showed me a flyer for the Peterborough Exhibition. Listed among the attractions–"Science Fair and Planetarium".

I hopped the next bus to the fairgrounds. I tore into the Recreation Centre. Representing Science were an ant farm and a model of Peterborough's hydraulic liftlock. A pâpier-maché sun dangled from a ceiling fan. Nine styrofoam orbs twirled around it.

The solar system.

"That's it?" I said punching my hip. "That's it?" I trudged out into the midway. Wall-to-wall people. Kids swarming the Haunted House, The Caterpillar, The Chairplane. The moon a fingernail clipping.

I staggered up against a cotton candy stand and shut my eyes. When I opened them I saw a dumbbell tilting in midair. It was cherry red, studded with lights. Instead of weights it had cages full of screaming people.

I fell onto my back, hands pillowing my head, heavenly bodies whirring across the sky.

EX

I started work at the Ex. I put up a fence around the petting zoo. I helped assemble game booths. The Funhouse came in one piece. They lifted it off the truck and plugged it in.

Mom's deep into gardening. Yesterday she tied stuffed animals to stakes and planted them around her vegetables.

*

My car's been acting up. The fan belt snapped and I replaced it with a pair of Mom's nylons. Next day the oil pan went.

Tonight I sold ride coupons. Didn't make it home till midnight. Dad worried my car had broken down. He lit a hundred citronella candles and waited on the stoop.

*

I drove Dad to Stuart Motors. He chose a camper. Apart from some rust on the axle it's in pretty decent shape. He and Mr. Johnson are going to take it on their trip.

We hitched it to the car. When we got home Mom stood in the driveway and watched us park. Dad got out. Mom stormed away.

At quarter to four I left for the fairgrounds. I came home to a dark house. The camper full of shadows. As I drove past it Dad waved. Then he blew out the candles.

*

For supper I ate candy apples, caramel corn, cotton candy. I helped folks onto the Zipper. The Zipper's like a Ferris wheel with cages that spin upside-down. All night I got pelted with coins and car keys. My gut aching.

*

In '49 Dad and Mr. Johnson travelled to Algonquin Park. In '50 they went to the Finger Lakes. Last summer it was the Appalachian mountains in Kentucky. You should see the photos. Hundred-foot gorges. Dad and Mr. Johnson skunked, arms around each other. Pup tent flapping in the wind.

*

No word from Dad. Mom visited me at work. We strolled through the Memorial Centre. All the prize flowers are wilted, the veggies dried-up. Blue-ribbon baking locked in the scorekeeper's cage.

I won two stuffed animals for Mom's garden.

*

Today they tore it down. The Jolly Caterpillar, The Salt-'n-Pepper Shaker, The Heartbreak Express. When the Conklin trucks had gone I swept the fairgrounds.

I got home at 11. The phone rang. When I picked it up the line was dead. Mom was on the stairs.

Go to bed, I said.

She just stared at me. She gathered the collar of her nightgown into a fist and held it there.

*

Mom's cornflowers are blooming. She gave me one to send you. I crushed it in a dictionary. Hope it gets there okay.

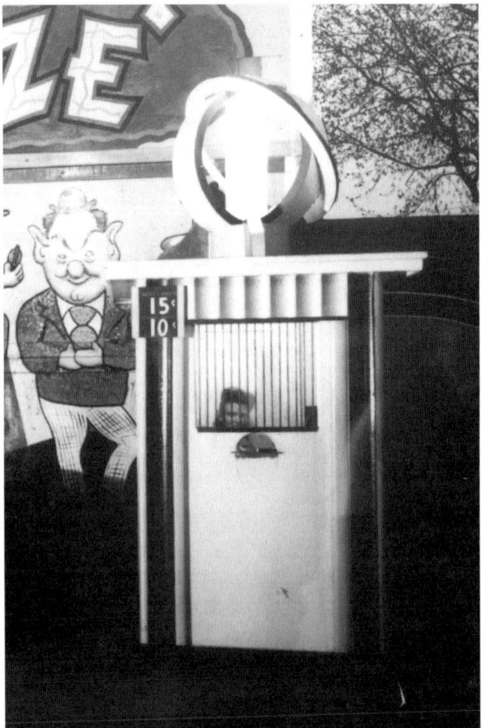
ZE
15¢
10¢

HARDWOOD

Rick picked me up at the cottage at sundown. We sped out onto the highway.

He was wearing jeans. Stroking my thigh I said, "Will linen pants be warm enough?"

"Here's the deal," he said. "You don't talk to me, I won't kill you."

Hayfields, churches, barns. By and by he pulled over by an insulbrick house. He said, "Get in back."

I did. A girl scurried up the drive. She was wearing denim too. She climbed in front and kissed Rick and we were off. Bog, pines, bog....

She twisted around. "You're Derek? Hi I'm Kathy. How do you know Rick?"

Rick answered. "His parents' place is next to ours. Mom made me bring him."

She squinted and smiled. "It'll be fun," she said. "Do you have a girlfriend?"

"I have no time for romance," I said. "In Toronto there's always so much to do. The theatre, ballet."

Rick grumbled and gunned through a town called Glen Alda. A Shell station and a sand dome. Two bulldozers dozing in the fairground.

"Did you get to the fair this year?" Kathy said. "We had great weather for it."

"I hate carnivals," I said. "They're so tawdry. Do you know what the CNE is?"

"Well I've never actually been...."

"Don't bother," I said. "The International Pavilion's the only thing worth seeing. Last year I bought sabots there. You know those wooden shoes Dutch people wear? Well they're *very* comfortable."

She massaged her nape. "Really?" she said. "I guess you know a lot about that stuff."

"I always get A's in Geography," I said.

We turned down a dirt road and crossed a meadow, parked with a half-dozen other cars at the base of a knoll. She grabbed blankets from the trunk. He fished a Mason jar out from under his seat.

"What's that?" I said.

"Know what whiskey is?" he said.

I followed them over the knoll to a falling field. They made for a bunch of kids circling a bonfire. I crouched nearby. Weeds and tallgrass shivering in the breeze.

I counted eighteen people. Two by two they started drifting into the field. Rick and Kathy vanished. A gang of newcomers arrived. One guy mingled his way around the blaze, swigging a beer. Bermuda shorts, baseball cap. Muscles.

I stared till he noticed me.

"Don't believe I know you," he said. He walked over and we shook. His name was Les. He asked who I'd come with and I told him.

"Oh yeah?" he said. "What'd they do take off with your booze?"

"No no," I said. "I hate alcohol. It kills brain cells."

"What's that supposed to mean?" he said. He spat at my feet and then swaggered toward the fire.

"Les wait I–"

Over his shoulder he flipped me the finger.

I rose and dusted my trousers and waded into the field. Burs on my socks. Mosquitoes bleeding my ankles. "Kathy?" I said. "Rick?"

I kicked Rick. In the ribs. He moaned, leapt up, a tepee of Y-front poking out of his fly.

"Get the fuck outta here!" he said.

Kathy flipped onto her stomach, her brassiere like a caterpillar tent in the grass.

"Oh God," I said, "I'm sorry I didn't know you were–"

"Git before I bust your fucking head!" he said.

I ran back to my patch by the fire. Now we were seven. I waved to Les. He whispered to a buddy. After a minute they rose and walked west into a thicket. They emerged clutching lumber. While they fed the flames I investigated.

Roots veined the trail. I crept forward, steadying myself on branches. Finally I came on a shack in a clearing. Two of its walls had been stripped away. On the ground lay a heap of tobacco tins and newspapers. Two-by-fours.

Tottering down the trail with two boards on my shoulder, two under my arm. I dropped them by the fire. Mouse turds on my clothes. Glasses streaked with sweat. I dried them off but Les had gone. Everyone had. Belches and giggles floating on the air.

I heaved a board into the fire.

The next board I heaved slid across the mound. Embers scattered into the tallgrass. The tallgrass took.

"Hey you guys!" I said.

Flames jumping blade to blade, weeds curling into red-hot filaments.

"Guys?" I said.

I dashed up the knoll. The blaze was burning in a V across the field. Smoke where trees should've been.

Far off someone shouted, "Fire!" Suddenly the smoke was full of shadows running and howling. Les loomed up and vanished. I bolted to the car. The keys were in it. I gunned up to the edge of the highway. A wall of pines one direction, same thing the other. A porcupine smeared on the dividing line.

WOW
YOU WILL
NEVER FORGET
YOU'LL
LIKE IT

BUOY

Bryan Benson did a cartwheel and a flip, then walked on his hands. The class clapped.

Coach called me up next. I crouched at the edge of the mat. I somersaulted. I somersaulted again. Then with a quarter-turn to the right I somersaulted twice more and stood, arms outspread. Spine paining.

"Whaddya call that?" Bryan said.

The guys laughed. Coach walked up to me. Pointing to my neck he said:

"What's that rash?"

*

Two weeks previous it had been a pimple. Then it had multiplied into a half-dozen nickel-sized blotches. The blotches became scales. When Coach saw them he phoned my Mom. Mom drove me to Peterborough that afternoon. A doctor at Nicholl's Hospital pricked my back with needles. He drew blood till my elbows were blue as blackberries.

*

With lupus the body's immune system attacks itself. The doctor admitted me and dosed me with penicillin twice a day. He kept my drapes drawn, to shield me from sunlight. And he injected me full of a steroid called hydrocortisone.

Word ripped through Nephton. My minister brought me a bottle of chlorophyll water. Schoolteachers brought chocolates. The Bensons visited once.

My body slathered in butter, wrapped in Saran.

Mrs. Benson smiled. "You're looking well."

Bryan snickered.

Mrs. Benson said, "Bryan got a job at Hiller's Marina for the summer."

"That's swell," I whispered.

*

During exam week I lay with ice packs on my knee and elbow joints. I celebrated my birthday by peeing into cups. At supper the nurses brought me a cupcake decorated with the number sixteen.

Then the blotches began to vanish. Just like that. By week's end my bones had stopped aching.

My doctor said:

"It'll be like this as long as you live. Flare and remit. Flare and remit."

Mom and Dad drove me home. Trees flowering. Buttercups on scrub land. "I think a celebration's in order," Dad said turning down Stoney Lake Road toward Hiller's Marina.

The lunchroom faced the lake. It was packed. The Reynolds, the Tuckers, the Greens–folks kept stopping by the table to ask how I felt. I smiled and nodded, eyeing the mirror on the wall. My bald crown. Sunken cheeks.

"Excuse me a sec," I said.

Grabbing a washroom key I stepped out onto the deck. A bunch of guys were sitting out there. Bryan included.

"Check out the bone rack," he said. "Hey how about a somersault?"

*

Come morning I hatched a Charles Atlas regimen. In my bedroom I did sit-ups, push-ups, stretches. When I told Mom I was going for a walk she said:

"Honey the sun."

My face slicked with petroleum jelly I took a walk through the bush behind the house. A couple hundred yards that first day, a couple hundred more the next. I skirted the nepheline syenite mine. I came on abandoned shafts flooded with greenish water, signs nailed to trees–CAUTION: NO SHALLOW AREA. I followed the train tracks of long-gone lumber camps.

After a couple weeks I made it to Stoney Lake.

*

In the morning I put trunks on under my trousers and told Mom I'd be gone a while. At Stoney Lake I stripped down and waded in. I did a breast-stroke at first, coaxing myself, breathe, stroke, breathe, stroke. I passed cottages, waves gurgled around docks. When my arms cramped I did the egg-beater with my legs. When my legs cramped I backstroked. When I cramped head to toe I treaded water.

Took me an hour to get there. I dragged myself onto the dock, gulping air. There were men sitting at picnic tables, filleting fish on newspaper. I staggered past, into the marina. Cold rippled from a fridge full of Coke. It soothed my sunburnt shoulders and neck.

"Bryan here?" I said.

I collapsed to the floor.

Two men carried me out to the side stoop and lay me on a bench. One fanned me. He said:

"You want me to find Bryan?"

I moaned and forced myself up onto my elbow. I tried to focus. Kids were winging softballs around. Minnows racing around bait shop bathtubs.

LOVE LIES DEEP

The man stalked down Seasonal and stashed a tin of shortbreads in his coat. I pursued him out the Simcoe St. exit.

"Excuse me sir," I said tapping his shoulder. "I work at Turnbull's and–"

Boom. He coldcocked me. I came to on the sidewalk.

When I got home I crushed ice for a compress. Uncle Trevor padded downstairs in pyjamas, cowlick standing on end.

"Long day huh?" he said.

"Yep."

"The other guy look as bad?"

"Yep."

He scooped a palmful of the ice into a tumbler. "Your problem is you're too scrawny. You should bulk up." He pushed up a sleeve and flexed his arm.

"That's a hundred push-ups every morning."

"Congratulations." I crossed into the family room and flicked the radio on. Bing Crosby.

I sank onto the sofa. Trevor appeared in the doorway, sipping a whiskey highball.

"Carol and I are heading downtown first thing," he said. "If you'd like to join us."

"Maybe."

He eased down beside me. Sweeping aside the compress he fingered my eyebrow.

I kissed his chin. I kissed his mouth and slid my hand under his top. Up to his nipple, down his treasure trail, past the knotted drawstring of his bottoms....

He gripped my wrist. "Sorry pal. I've already had it tonight."

"Well go for the record," I whispered.

"Good idea." He stood and shook off my hand. "I'll go see if Carol's up to it."

"I was joking," I said. "Just sit down."

I grabbed at his leg. He dodged me, then sauntered to the staircase in the hall. Highball sloshing.

"You be a good boy," he said, "and we'll see what Santa brings."

"Fuck you."

He smirked and disappeared upstairs. Bing crackling on the radio.

I shut him off and turned in.

*

The sky spat all next morning. Trevor let Carol off at Market Hall. I volunteered to go with her.

"Thanks hon," she said, "but I was hoping you'd take him for a shave."

"Aw she loves it," he said winking at me and scratching the shadow on his chin.

Straight razor, lavender foam. He tipped the barber a buck and we walked toward Turnbull's, navigating slush puddles and sandwich boards and Santas from the Sally Ann.

He said, "What do you think Carol'd like for Christmas?"

"How should I know?" I said.

I tailed him through the perfume and jewelry departments. In Ladies' Wear he picked up a floral housedress.

"No no no," I said. "Try a nice bathrobe. Or slippers."

"You try it," he said. "I need coffee."

*

Trevor and Carol gave me an electric razor. "What is it?" he kept asking as I unwrapped it. He gave her a silk blouse and a White Shoulders bath assortment. Thirty percent off with my discount.

"Trevor they're perfect," Carol said.

*

The house shifting under frost. The groaning

staircase. Trevor stole into the room and crawled up my bed. He reeked of whiskey.

"Hey," he said.

I turned away. "Fuck off," I said.

He squeezed my leg. "Where's your Christmas spirit?" he said and kissed the back of my neck.

I rolled over and unbuttoned his pyjamas. While I blew him I fingered his asshole. That way his smell stayed with me for days.

He came, then jerked me off.

I scurried to the bathroom, returning on tiptoe with tissues. "Want one?" I said.

My window rattled. Across the field lights blinked in an upside-down V.

"Trevor," I said. "Trevor wake up," I said. I eased down beside him. I kissed his throat. Then I started sucking it, busting veins, a bruise the shape of my mouth blooming beneath his skin.

HANDS

This year Kelly asked her parents to send her to the world trapshooting championship in Vandalia Ohio. The Grand American Handicap, it's called.

"I can take the bus," she said. "It'll hardly cost anything."

Mrs. Forrest said, "Honey I'm not sure trapshooting's the sort of sport you should be involved in."

She clamped her hands on her hips. "Oh really?" she said. "And what is?"

Mrs. Forrest suggested ballet.

*

Kelly drove to my house and we walked downtown. Dandelions bursting from cracks in the cement.

"I can give you twenty bucks," I said.

She smiled, punched my arm. We stopped in at every store on George Street. Silver's Shoes and Walkwel's both needed summer help. On the street she told me she'd rather die than touch people's feet.

"Anyway," she added, "my folks would find me at Walkwel's."

We wandered up to the clock tower and south on Charlotte, ducking into Hampton's Novelty to buy Marlboros. Kelly asked Mr. Hampton if he had anything available.

"What do you know about gags?" he said.

"What do you wanna know?"

He folded his arms. "I don't pay much."

"Then I won't strain myself."

He hired her part-time.

*

Mr. Hampton kept a candy counter crammed with Hands fireworks. Bombardos, maroons, mines. Kelly discovered a false bottom in a drawer of Burning Schoolhouses. Hidden below were packets of powder. RED SPARKS, BLUE SPARKS, GOLD TWINKLES.

"What are these for?" she said.

"Mind your own business," he said.

*

Kelly dumped a bag of fireworks on my deck. She pulled a jackknife out of her pocket, slit a Roman candle and sliced away the wrapping. Eight aggie-sized balls on a bed of black powder. "Stars," she said. "They flare in midair." Next she slit a Fountain. Same kind of casing but a half-inch wider nozzle. "Just like a gun," she said. "The fuller the choke the farther the stuff flies."

*

Next weekend she brought over twenty batons wrapped in kraft. "Paper towel tubes," she said running her fingers over a baton. "The powder's from Dad's shells."

We wrapped them in white tissue and brainstormed names. She liked "Stiff Shooters" and "Exploding Parents". I painted the names onto the shafts in gold.

*

I parked on the shoulder of the highway, propped our HOMEMADE FIREWORKS sign against the trunk. A half-mile south Kelly lit a Fountain. A gold zipper against the denim-coloured sky. Cars slowed to look. By the time she'd jogged down to meet me I'd sold out of stock.

*

Dip wires in shellac and steel filings. *Presto!*– sparklers. Kelly sealed them in sandwich bags, four to a pack.

We launched them near the swimming hole on River Road. She held a Stiff Shooter in her hands, blasted stars at passing boats.

A car with Ohio plates pulled over. Two guys in shorts and tee-shirts stepped out. "Your friend's crazy," one guy said.

"Do you guys know where Vandalia is?" I said.

They asked why and I motioned to Kelly. She was loping toward us, hair blackened where she tucks it behind her ears.

"You a trapshooter?" shouted one guy.

"I used to be," she said. "Now I'm a pyrotechnician!"

She copied the addresses of motels and restaurants in Vandalia. She asked the guys for their phone numbers.

"You gonna tell your parents?" I said.

"I'll mail them a post card when I get there," she said.

*

Dominion Day I posted myself in a turnaround between Bridgenorth and Lakefield. She stood by a PLEASE DON'T LITTER sign, trying to light a candle. Twice the breeze blew out her Zippo. Finally the quickmatch caught.

So did her sweatshirt. She tumbled to the gravel. I screamed. The candle whistled onto the road and *bang!*–copper blazed blue, cryolite and barium chlorate fused into purple, charcoal exploded in gold streamers. The blacktop melting beneath.

I found her in a ditch, submerged up to her face in dead water. The ambulance guys told me they'd contact her parents. A policeman jotted down my name and address.

"Don't go far," he said.

CATTLE CALL

Eric brought me a cowboy shirt to wear. It was black with white stitching and snaps instead of buttons.

Uncle Jamie stopped me on my way out the door. "You know the rules," he said. "No alcohol. Play today pay tomorrow."

The water tank atop Quaker Oats was floodlit. Ditto city hall and the courthouse.

"Here's my place." Eric cruised by a redbrick building. The Red Dog Hotel. "Not bad huh?"

We blew through Peterborough and in no time we'd arrived. He parked by a dumpster. He checked his hair in the rearview.

Tex Ritter singing "Blood on the Saddle". Wood shavings on the floor. While he went for beers I grabbed a booth. Half standing I scoped around. There were a few leaning on the bar, a few two-stepping with boyfriends. A doll in a scoop top by the juke.

Eric came back with a girl. “This here’s Mr. Walter’s nephew,” he said. “I’m showing him the ropes this summer.”

“Yeah?” She tapped a smoke against her pack. Orange nails.

We washed the beer down with whiskey. I held it all in till my dick was piss-hard. Teetering at the urinal with one arm bracing the wall, a flystrip twirling overhead. Eric fumbled with my hind pocket.

“Here’s the keys,” he said. “Ask her for a walk.”

She said sure. Trying to keep a poker face I snaked behind her through the crowd. Eric and two strangers were hallooing me and flashing thumbs up from a different booth. I turned and flipped them the bird just before passing outside.

“Nice night eh?” I said.

“Real nice,” she said. “Wanna sit in the pickup?”

We locked the doors and cranked the windows up. She moved close.

“You smell beautiful,” I said.

She laughed and stroked me from knee to thigh. My throat gurgled. When she kissed me it gurgled again.

“Sorry I–”

“It’s all right.” She tongued my lips and we frenched. A flick of her hand undid my belt. My zipper. She hunched and husked my shorts and my dick curled out, come gummed at the tip.

“Is it okay?” I said.

"Sshh." She choked it down. After a couple swallows the suction was strong enough. Bang.

Between gasps I thanked her.

"No problem," she said adjusting her bobby pins.

*

Around 4 I snuck to the bathroom and beat off. I still had blue balls come daybreak. The buffalo bawling and rumbling in off the western fields. Jamie was dropping hay bales and salt licks from the flatbed. I tucked in my sheets and bounded downstairs to the kitchen.

Saturdays forenoon Jamie and Dar peddle meat in town at Market Hall. After breakfast I helped pack coolers and went with them. We set up in a stall by the Charlotte St. entrance. On the counter we displayed a buffalo doll and a placard picturing which cuts come from which parts of the animal. Round and loin and rump roasts sold out first. When business died off Jamie let me go.

I wandered the aisles sampling freebies, maple fudge and peaches and curds. One farmer had a daughter my age working. I lined up in front of her.

"One cuke please," I said.

"One?"

"Yep." I stared at her lips, the freckles on her nose.

She smiled and shrugged and passed me my purchase. "Five cents."

I gave her a quarter. "Keep the change."

Candy carts and souvenir stands dotted Market Square. I bought a post card of George St. "Dear Mom and Dad sorry I haven't written blah blah blah." I walked to Jaye's Variety for a stamp. Two bobbysoxers were scarfing down jujubes outside.

"Hi there," I said.

"Do I know you?" said one girl. A redhead. Built.

"I'm Derek."

"And I'm Lily-Jo-Mae."

Her friend giggled and scraped her sandal along the cement.

"Fresh off the farm?" said red.

I hid the cucumber behind my back.

*

We topped up our thermoses and took off through the stock gate into the compound. Clay then chess then scrub. The buffalo were clustered to the east, scratching themselves against silver birches. Scrolls of bark clung to their fur.

Spring runoff had stripped and gullied topsoil. Fence posts across the northern boundary had tipped. Eric and I righted them, tamped soil around the bases. Shirts stuffed in our waistbands, skin scorching. The tattoo on his arm faded to the green colour of his pants.

*

Coyotes cried through the night. Dogs and birds answering back. I was up at dawn. Jamie filled the feed bins and we waited. Bulls appeared first, two tons apiece including horns. None missing. Next came cows trailed by their young. As he counted calves his face fell.

"You lads keep an eye out," he said. "And take traps."

I dug some number four and a halfs out of the shed. After lubing them with lard I bagged them in burlap sacks padded with spruce and balsam twigs. Eric arrived and I told him what Jamie'd said.

"Figured that." He loaded the flatbed and climbed behind the wheel. We drove in silence toward the woods that stretched beyond the ranch's northern boundary. He flipped his visor and a pouch of Red Man tumbled to his lap. He offered me a plug. I accepted.

He downshifted. "Lookit."

Three blobs cropped out of the hardscrabble. Two were turkey buzzards. They eyed us, then turned and spread their wings and laboured skyward.

He parked and we hopped out.

"Jesus." I pinched my nose. The calf was a shell of fur and bone and blackflies. Stringy guts webbed the ground.

He kicked at a hoof. "Might as well set friggin' mousetraps. What we need's poison. Poison meat. The mother'd eat it and puke it up for the cubs and then they'd all die."

He hawked his chaw.

*

I lit out toward town, then hung a right at Brealey Drive but nothing seemed familiar. I turned down a county road and the asphalt tapered into a single dirt lane. A man was torching tent caterpillars that had nested in roadside trees. I asked for directions and he sketched a map in the sand.

At Benny's two drunks were duking it out on the dance floor. The bouncer waited ringside, baseball bat in hand. I scouted around for Eric. Five or six bodies were sardined into each booth. I spotted two guys I remembered meeting. Or seeing.

"Hey," I said. "You seen Eric Beech?"

"Who wants to know?" one of them said.

"I'm the guy from the other night, the one with the lady."

"Oh the one with the *lady*. Now I recognize you." He patted the plank beside him.

I sat.

"I'm Dwight, this is Reg."

"Good to know you," I said.

"You're sure dressed to kill."

"What're you drinking?" said Reg.

"Anything," I said, "if someone'll get it for me."

I gave him a sawbuck and he bought a tray of shooters. We shotgunned them all. Ditto round two.

Dwight tipped a glass against my lips. "Bottoms up cowboy."

"Had enough." I boxed air and tried to stand but the booze rushed my brain. One foot caught the table post and I tumbled from the booth. Catcalls and applause from the crowd. Dwight and Reg shouldered me to the lot. I said, "I think you better take me home."

They were already rooting through my pockets for keys.

Curled up in the back seat, clothes battered in sawdust and sweat. One of the guys uncapped a mickey and the fumes flooded my nostrils. Vomit lumped in my throat. I heard radio, the turn signal, gravel under the tires. When I tried to say stop I retched again. Finally Dwight braked. I scrambled out and puked twice on the same patch of bluebells.

I rolled over to find them emptying the trunk. Jugs of washer fluid, Dar's mackinaw, tire chains arced through the air. I bent my legs to rise. Reg knocked me back.

"Not yet cowboy," he said.

Save for far-off forks of lightning everything beyond the headlights was dark. A ridge of spiky treetops. Dwight uncovered a crowbar and carried it over.

"Take off your clothes."

I teared. "What are you gonna do?"

He whacked my arm. "Shut up and give them."

I worked my right boot off. Then my left.

Reg crouched and popped open my shirt. Next he unbuttoned my jeans and yanked them off. My shorts came off too. "Lift your feet," he said.

I cupped my dick.

He squinted at me a sec. “You little fucker....”

I flipped over and jackknifed my legs to sprint. A boot stamped me to the ground.

“You calling us fags? You calling us fags?”

The tip of the crowbar struck my tailbone. I gasped and writhed and shielded my rear with my hands. Dwight kicked them away.

“You want it up the ass?” He jabbed there and missed. He jabbed again.

I pressed fingers to my hole and they came up slick and black.

The car roared off in a squall of dust and pebbles. I weaved toward the taillights, sobbing, guts aflame.

Somewhere something howled. I howled back.

'CRYSTAL MAZE'
MAISON aux MIROIRS
CRYSTAL MAZE
CRYSTAL MAZE

MEN WITH BROKEN HEARTS

THIS WEEKEND–HANK WILLIAMS AND HIS DRIFTING COWBOYS!

I tore the poster off the lamppost, then ran home and taped it to my bedroom wall. I phoned my friend Michael. I begged Dad to lend me money for a ticket.

He offered me a deal. He'd buy tickets for me and Michael. In exchange we'd clean an old hunting camp he'd bought.

"Hunting is so barbaric," I said.

*

First thing next morning Michael and I headed north in Dad's truck. Hank bursting through radio static.

"Whaddya think he'll open with?" Michael said.

"'Lovesick Blues'. For sure. That's his signature song."

The driveway teemed with wild oat and pine saplings. It led to a frame cabin in a clearing. We found a two-seater outhouse. A rabbit bobbing in a lidless well.

"This is so disgusting," I said.

He scythed the yard, I swept the cabin. Shotgun shells, mouse turds, newspapers from the 30's. DEPRESSION CONTINUES, DEPRESSION DEEPENS. I chucked it all. The linoleum peeling in every corner. A square behind the stove lifted up entirely. I spied a chain hooked to the floor. I yanked it. The floor creaked open.

"Michael!"

He crept down the ladder. I tagged after. The root cellar was about six feet long though it wasn't much wider than his shoulders. Clay walls. Rotten potatoes underfoot.

"What do you think?" he said. "Get a couple girls down here, some candles...."

"Are you joking?" I said pinching my nose. "It's *putrid*!"

*

That evening at home I worked on my shirt, a white Stay-Press short-sleeved number. With a pencil I sketched two half-notes over the breast pockets. I smeared glue between the lines and poured a bag of emerald sequins over top.

Dad came in and frowned. I told him that Hank's shirts and blazers had fringed cuffs and yokes, beaded horseshoes and lassos, iron-on guitar decals. One jacket sported the first two bars of "Lovesick Blues", the musical notation in royal piping, the lyrics in aqua rhinestones.

*

The following day Michael and I shingled and painted for eight hours. After dining on baked beans and chicken we unrolled sleeping bags and bedded down on the cabin floor, our transistor blasting.

"Next," said the D.J., "we'll be cooking something up with Mr. Hank Williams."

I whooped and clapped.

"You think he's in town?" Michael said.

"Probably tomorrow."

"Where do you figure he'll stay?"

"Princess Gardens maybe. Maybe the Holiday Inn." I curled up on my side. Smoke coiling off a Pic. On the radio: "Hey Good Lookin'".

Michael kissed my neck.

I sat up like a shot. "What are you doing?"

"I thought maybe...."

I gaped at him.

"I'm better looking than Hank."

"You're a fruit!"

"What about you?" he said. "What about your shirt?" He stared at me a moment. Then he got up, put on his jeans and stalked out of the cabin.

"Where are you going? Michael?"

The truck engine drowned me out. I dashed outside. Taillights shrank and died away.

*

At daybreak I tramped to the road. Eyelids flagging. A family in a Monarch picked me up. They took me to the Jack's Lake Marina and I phoned home from there.

Dad came to get me. His cowlick standing on end, pyjama top tucked into jeans. We returned to camp. No Michael.

"You've got ten seconds to tell me what the hell is going on," Dad said.

I said I didn't know.

"People just don't pack up and leave! Were you drinking? Was he sneaking off to see some girl?"

*

We combed Peterborough. The Victory Grill, the Greeks restaurant, the lookout up on Armour Hill. On every lamppost a poster–TONIGHT! DIRECT FROM THE GRAND OLE OPRY! ONE SHOW ONLY! We drove to Michael's place. I explained to his parents that he'd disappeared during the night.

"But he'll be back by seven," I said. "He won't miss Hank."

They all scowled. Dad said, "You can damn well forget Hank."

The sky was streaked with pink as we set out for home. I flipped the radio on and caught the tail end of "Window Shopping".

Dad flipped it off. "I'm gonna call the cops," he said.

A siren shut him up. By Market Hall he pulled over to let a police cruiser pass. Tailing the cruiser was a Ford Packard with Alabama plates. In the back sat a man in a ten-gallon hat.

I jumped from the car. I raced down Charlotte Street, behind the Bell Building. Half a block from the Brock Ballroom I heard a guitar twang. I snatched a ticket from my wallet. Panting I fought my way through the foyer and across the dance floor and up to the stage. The Drifting Cowboys were tuning, uniformed in black trousers and cowboy shirts. With a one-two-three they launched into the intro to "Lovesick Blues".

Hank stepped from the wings. He was taller than me, skinnier. Hunched up like a bass clef.

My eyes filled. I threw my arms up.

Then he fell. His knees buckled and he flopped onto his guitar. Struggling up he staggered to the mike. "Fuckin' fuckin' fuck," he said. The band repeated the intro. Hank glared offstage. When he fell again he took the mike stand with him. His hat rolled off, a white Stetson, sweatband yellowed.

I reached for it.

"Get away!" A man scooted onstage and

grabbed the hat. He went over and lifted Hank by the shoulders. The bassist lifted Hank's feet.

Hank waved.

TOILET

PASSING ON

Hair is dead protein the body ejects. Chris plucks a strand from his head. It's blond. I take off my glass-es and examine it under the microscope.

"Atoms are the basic units of everything. They're so small they're invisible yet they pack enough power to kill." This is what our teacher told us.

Four weeks Grandpa lay in the hospital, lungs turning to pus. Doctors pumped him full of peni-cillin. Nothing helped.

*

I boxed up the things in Grandpa's den. In a cedar chest crammed with papers I discovered a note from his grandmother signed "L.S. McCormick".

"When Grandpa was twenty," Dad said, "he

changed the ‘i’ in his surname to ‘a’. He thought it looked less Catholic that way.”

*

I meet Chris in the school foyer so I can walk into the locker room with him. I change in a stall in the washroom. When I come out he’s in his BVD’s, brown tufts furring his armpits. Nipples.

*

When I was six Grandpa gave me a brush and a razor without a blade so I could pretend to shave. My top lip was the first place I got hair. “It’s just peach fuzz,” he said. He warned me that once I started shaving my beard would grow out stubbly. That’s how my pubic hair came in. One or two strands at a time. I trimmed them every night.

*

The undertaker never met Grandpa before he embalmed him. This explains why at his wake Grandpa’s hair was parted on the left side not the right. Otherwise he looked good. Face powdered, lips rouged. Belly full of an astringent that cooked his organs.

*

In October our Science teacher takes our class on an overnight field trip. He teaches us tricks for surviving in Nature–how to start a fire without matches, how to build a lean-to out of twigs. Everyone makes a pinbox camera and photographs the woods. I point mine at Chris. He won't stand still for ten minutes. When the picture comes out it's blurry.

*

My family formed a receiving line at Grandpa's wake. Before passing the casket folks would shake hands with me and Dad and hug my mom and sister. "What fine looking children," they'd say. And to me: "You look so much like your father."

*

Grandpa phoned my mother at the hospital right after my sister was born. "Good stuff," he said, "but you're going to have to try again." When I was delivered he said, "That's more like it. Keep the McCormack name alive."

*

Campfire songs at 9, marshmallows at 9:30. Boys and girls retire to separate cabins. I change into pyjamas in the bathroom. Chris and I flip a quarter for the top bunk. I get bottom.

Just after midnight someone knocks at the

window. Chris jumps down and opens it. The other guys are either sleeping or pretending to sleep. I hold my breath. Even when someone steps on my arm climbing into the top bunk, I still hold my breath.

The boards above me begin to creak. Whispers I can't understand. I get out of bed and look. I can see Chris, his arms and shoulders. Her hand on the back of his head.

*

Eons ago one microbe attacked another and engulfed it. Made the other one a part of itself. The result was a new microbe, stronger and with a longer life span. "This," said our teacher, "was the first example of sexual intercourse." Which sheds light on a lot of things. Pneumonia. Gangrene. Atrophy. Putrefy. Corrupt. Different names for the same thing.

*

Chris showed up at Grandpa's wake in suit and tie. I excused myself from the line. We snuck out the back door and sat on the steps. He put his arm around my shoulders. I rested my head against his neck. His aftershave smelled like lilacs. I shivered accidentally.

"It's okay," he whispered. "It's okay."

The WINNAH!
It's the Cats

PHOTO CREDITS

Cover photograph
London Free Press Collection of
Photographic Negatives
The D.B. Weldon Library
The University of Western Ontario
London, Ontario N6A 3K7

Pages 10, 20 and 94
Courtesy Peterborough Agricultural Society

Pages 14, 26, 58, 64 and 99
Courtesy Herschell Carrousel Factory Museum/
Carousel Society of the Niagara Frontier

Pages 36, 42, 48, 52, 70, 76 and 86
Courtesy Records and Archives of Exhibition Place,
Toronto